To
Allison &
Gabrielle,
May all your
dreams come true,

Katherine Duffly

7-27-12
Old Faithful Inn
Yellowstone N.P.

# Beauregart the Bear

Written by **Kathryn Phyllarry**

Illustrated by **Robert Rath**

**Homestead Publishing**

Moose, WY • San Francisco, CA

In memory of my parents, Phyllis and Harry, for whom I write.

For my daughters, Nicole and Lindsey, with whom the learning process has been mutual over the years.

And for my husband, and soul mate, Jim with his constant words: "That's a great start; keep writing."

Copyright © 2009 by Kathryn Rittmueller

Book design by Robert Rath

ISBN 978-09-943972-80-0

Library of Congress Control Number 2009926820

First Edition
Printed in China

Published by
Homestead Publishing
Box 193 • Moose, Wyoming 83012
& San Francisco, California 94114

For other fine Homestead titles, please contact:
Mail Order Department
Homestead Publishing
Box 193 • Moose, Wyoming 83012
or www.homesteadpublishing.net

**B**eauregart the bear was born

on a very cold January morning.

This young cub's life would make its mark

in a place called Yellowstone National Park.

His mother woke briefly from her long winter's nap

and cuddled him closely in her lap.

At birth, Beau only weighed one pound,

which was the common weight for a new born around.

His mother was hibernating for the winter,

but little Beau's birth this would not hinder.

**W**hile licking him clean in the den's dim light,

she noticed his left front paw wasn't right.

She continued to examine him from paws to snout,

and he was healthy beyond a doubt.

His mother grunted, "The love I have

for you my baby boy

nothing will ever destroy.

You are going to be strong my little love,

sure as the stars shine above."

She closed off the den's opening with her back,

so Beau's protection wouldn't lack.

**B**eau's mother went back to sleep,

    but a close guard she would keep.

With him lying next to her fur,

    she could constantly feel his every stir.

Her body would always keep him content

    until Yellowstone's harsh winter was spent.

She would wake herself now and then

to make sure he was safe in the den.

For three months, she kept Beau warm and dry

and listened for his every cry.

In April, winter finally broke,

and from her sleep, Beau's mother woke.

Seven months without any food

  could certainly put a bear in a very hungry mood.

In winter, her body provided all of their needs,

  but now Beau's mother needed to feed.

There were many things in the forest to eat

  but the spring grasses were very sweet.

His mother's feeding trips became longer

as Beau grew stronger.

**S**he would race back to him without saying a word

if any strange sounds in the forest she heard.

In May, the pair left their winter home,

and, for the summer, they would roam.

Beau's left front paw wouldn't work,

and he kept falling down and getting hurt.

His mother would always stay very near

until his footing became secure.

They came to a meadow on their way

where other mothers and cubs were spending the day.

The other cubs came up to play,

but, when they saw Beau's paw, they ran away.

**A**ll they could do was sit and stare,

and left little Beau just standing there.

As the other cubs played and romped about,

little Beau was always left out.

Suddenly, a smell in the air

warned the mothers of danger out there.

**A**fternoon play was quickly shattered

as the mothers with their cubs franticly scattered.

Into tall pines, the young cubs climbed and on pine

nuts, for a while, would dine.

The other mothers and cubs good shelters could find,

but Beau and his mother were left behind.

Beau couldn't run very well you see,

and it was hard for them to flee.

**H**e could not climb trees like the other cubs

because his one paw was just a stub.

**W**olves looking for something to eat

were scouting out the very weak.

**A** challenge this would be, his mother knew in a glance,

with Beau's paw he didn't have a chance.

Beau's mother made a brave attack

knowing the intentions of the pack.

His mother fought hard and never gave in —

despite the fact she got a bite on the chin.

Those wolves scattered with

their heads and tails hanging down;

if they wanted to find food, it would be on other ground.

Mother bear grunted to her cub,

"There is a very big lesson to be learned here my dear;

you will have to be strong and from danger steer."

"**D**on't let your emotions about your paw run away,

simply let determination rule your day."

The pair headed to the river to fish and drink,

and this gave Beau time to think.

He couldn't let his future seem dim

simply because of his different limb.

**A**t the river's edge,

he made a pledge.

He would have to let go of the pity within

before his life could truly begin.

He would never again be someone's prey,

and it was going to begin today.

So into the water he went with a swish

determined that he would catch a fish.

Beau's mother guided him to the rivers pool

where the fish usually gathered as a rule.

"**B**e patient," she groaned, "and stand very still,

just pay close attention and develop your skill."

Beau found that fishing was harder than it looked until he used his paw as a hook.

**S**oon the other mothers and cubs arrived;

they were very surprised little Beau was alive.

While the other cubs were losing fish left and right,

Beau could hold onto a fish good and tight.

**"T**his paw is actually coming in handy," he thought,

"I am catching more fish than anyone's caught."

Beau's mother sat watching with her mouth in a smile;

she hadn't felt this much pride in quite a while.

**B**eau caught so many fish

that he shared them with others,

all the cubs and their mothers.

With their bellies full, Beau's mother could detect

that Beau had finally gained the others' respect.

**T**o little Beau, no one could be mean;

he was by far the best fishing bear they had ever seen.

**T**hrough the summer

Beau got stronger and learned how to run;

on three legs not four, which was actually sort of fun.

The cubs would have races

and Beau would take the lead;

somehow he developed a lot of speed.

**H**e found that life wasn't a bore;

   there were oh so many things a bear could explore.

Having the right mind set was the key

   to being anything he wanted to be.

With all of his frustrations beat,

   Beau found there were many goals to meet.

When fall arrived the pair needed more sleep,

as nature's clock said, there was an appointment to keep.

The geese were flying towards the border

    as the nights got cold and the days got shorter.

The warm weather quickly came to an end,

    and Beau and his mother needed to make a den.

This would most likely be the last year

    she would ever have her little Beau near.

In a hollow log they made their den

not far from the rivers bend.

Because Beau couldn't rake leaves with his paw,

a new way to make a den he saw.

He would bite off branch tips with his teeth

and lay them on the ground beneath.

Then he picked the tips up in his mighty jaws

and never had to use his paws.

**T**hey were active less and less each day

until Beau and his mother were in the den to stay.

**W**ith their heads between their paws

and their very warm pelts,

the two would sleep until the snow began to melt.

When the second winter in Beau's life broke,

mother and son finally awoke.

This time Beau would leave his mother's den

   never to return again.

His mother knew Beau was strong

   and would truly live a life that was long.

At the river one sunny summer morning,

she saw the bear that was her first born.

Beau was catching fish and sharing them with others,

and she was by far the proudest mother.

As Beau's mother was standing there,

watching him with a loving stare,

**S**he heard something that left her stunned,

and she knew what a good job Beau had done.

**A** little cub snorted,

   "That's Beau the bear with the paw that's not right."

The cub's mother grunted, "No, that's Beauregart

   the bear that's all heart."

**K**athryn (Jensen) Rittmueller, whose pseudonym is Kathryn Phyllarry, was born and raised in St. Paul, Minnesota. She and her husband Jim are outdoor enthusiasts who have lived in Wyoming for more than 30 years.